INNER CONFLICTS

INNER CONFLICTS

Remya V. Menon

ZORBA BOOKS

ZORBA BOOKS

Published in India by Zorba Books, 2017

Website: www.zorbabooks.com
Email: info@zorbabooks.com

ISBN Print Book - 978-93-86407-20-7
ISBN eBook - 978-93-86407-21-4

Zorba Books Pvt. Ltd.(opc)
Gurgaon, INDIA

Printed at : Repro Knowledgecast Limited, Thane

Dedication

To the memory of my Father,
who continues to be my teacher, guide and inspiration.

To my dearest Mother,
who keeps demonstrating her virtuousness in everyday life
and whose love for me is beyond words.

To my beloved friend, Priyanka,
who is a source of goodness and encouragement.

Acknowledgements

I am grateful to Zorba Books for publishing my book and making my dream a reality.

I am glad to thank my mother, Dr. Indira Vijayakumar, the first person to read and review the manuscript, for her enormous support and encouragement. That has driven me to get this humble work published.

I express my heartfelt thanks to my uncle, Mr. Kesava Dev, for his powerful blessings, guidance and support for this small endeavour.

I am happy to express my gratitude to my friend, Alexina Retna Priyanka, who has helped and encouraged me from the beginning. She has inspired me by her own passion for words.

I am immensely grateful to my friend, Veena Upadhya, for her suggestions regarding the book, her constant support and for being as excited about this little book as I am!

Thanks to all my family and friends who have always valued me and have led me to undertake many a venture such as this one!

Preface

I have observed that being idealistic or unconventional in our society can be challenging. It could be impractical. Although we have a lot to be thankful for in our lives, there are some inner battles most of us fight. Embarking on a new venture can be tough and frustrating. Progressive views may be frowned upon. People who are different in any way may find themselves conflicted. Corruption and unfairness might stand in your way. Women have to strive hard in order to be taken seriously. My idea for this book originated from this insight.

This novelette is built on a reflection of certain realities. The young characters in this story deal with their inner conflicts and the real world. They realise that swimming against the tide is arduous. They want to pursue their true calling, but without hurting their loved ones. This seems to be an almost impossible situation. Which path do they choose? What is the price they pay for it? Will they really succeed in their mission?

This short tale is set in India; it is mainly intended for the Indian reader. However, parts of it could be connected to the emotions and experiences of unconventional youth in any society. You may be able to relate to some of the incidents in the book. I do hope you enjoy it!

CHAPTER I

$\mathcal{P}$rem sat in the cafeteria gazing into the distance; the sun was still too bright to look at. It was another quiet evening after an uneventful day of work at the multinational corporation he was part of. Through the window he could see the beautiful flowerbeds bordering the carefully groomed lawns, as well as the edge of the swimming pool. He was inside the organisation's sprawling campus situated not far from one of India's most well-known metropolitan cities. Taking a sip of his drink, he mused about his life in Bangalore.

Prem was in his mid-twenties, bright and idealistic. His employers hadn't failed to take notice of his intellect and earnestness either. Evaluating his initial performance following a psychometric analysis, they had transferred him to their prestigious Research & Development wing. Within three years, he was working on major technical projects and leading entire teams. There was something astute in the way he coordinated and motivated his teammates. His concern for them was genuine and he nurtured all their ideas and talents. His superiors knew he would make his way up the corporate ladder rapidly.

He smiled to himself. He was quite successful in the eyes of his friends, colleagues and family. And yes, he liked his job here; it was innovative, the pay was good and he got ample recognition for his work. Still there was something nagging him, for this was not what his heart had wanted.

Hailing from a middle-class family in Kerala, he had been brought up and educated there. He hadn't wanted to take up engineering for graduation in the first place; it was his father's choice. He would have preferred to opt for a degree in social work. His parents opposed it, saying the scope for career growth was lean. A majority of Indian parents thought so indeed, engineering or medicine being the favoured and safe choice; it somehow brought a sense of security and certainty. Maybe it was the 'in' thing, perchance an indicator of social status. Probably they were scared to explore new horizons and risk their children's career. Prem, in his teens, yielded, partly because he didn't have a concrete opinion then. And of course, he loved his parents; a noble son, he would agree to their choices in order to make them happy. Yet there was another reason for his decision - Ramesh. The very thought of him brought a smile to Prem's lips. Ramesh was Prem's elder brother, whom he dearly loved, trusted and relied upon. He was a civil engineer by profession. Right from childhood, he had been a guide and companion to Prem.

Ramesh had persuaded his little brother that engineering would provide plenty of opportunities and that he could pursue his passion along with that. Almost all Ramesh's views were practical and foresighted. So Prem gladly gave in. Now, years later, he felt the decision was not bad after all.

Prem got to his feet and walked outside. The setting sun spread brilliant streaks of hue in the sky. The gathering twilight seemed soothing to him. Nothing like going back to nature! His thoughts were wandering again. A few months after graduation he had been offered a good job in an MNC, which he was, however, reluctant to accept. It would have been a dream job to many. But he had always wished to take up social service as a profession. Even when he was small, he was deeply pained by the suffering of people as well as the plight of animals that were tortured around him. The daily news hurt him, making him feel responsible to act in some way. His family, naturally, had other plans for a bright career and future for their progeny.

He strolled on, ignoring the mosquitoes settling on his forearms and hands. Prem would never hit a mosquito, intending harm to no creature whatsoever. He was inspired by the Buddhist and Jain principles. He remembered his mother telling him playfully, "You let them hurt you! Don't be such a saint!" But she was very proud of him.

As he grew up, he realised that practising total *Ahimsa* was impractical and even impossible; you couldn't sustain your life without harming a few organisms, however unintentionally; one could only minimise the damage that one caused to the world around; one could only minimise one's carbon footprint.

Sensing he was uncertain about the job, Ramesh had assured him, "This is something you can focus your creative energies on. Moreover, you are young and ought to go out and see the world. *Experience it*." Again, Prem was happy to oblige. Nevertheless, he decided that a part of his time, energy and savings would be reserved for charitable work.

As Ramesh had predicted, Prem did experience the world indeed. He interacted with a lot of smart people, made friends with his colleagues and spent many a night partying. He played tennis, drank beer, set out on long drives with pals, had a lot of fun and enjoyment. But after a while, it became routine, the pleasure from the activities waned away and he was troubled again.

He stepped into the lounge of his posh living quarters and took the elevator to his floor. Everything here was high-tech, which was something he appreciated. Inside the room, he splashed cold water on his face. He looked in the mirror at his receding hairline and somewhat jagged teeth, which people sometimes made fun of. He was tall and of average build. His unruly black hair did little to hide his balding head. As he stood there staring at his image, he found himself facing the same conflict yet again, "Is this really what I want to do?"

CHAPTER II

Prem was walking along the corridor of his plush office building chatting with his colleagues. He had been racking his brains all morning, trying to resolve a particularly tricky technical issue. It was like playing the computer game, Conundrum, he pondered. You try to raise one set of blocks and the other side goes down. It was tough to get everything right simultaneously.

He could feel the beginnings of a headache. He often wondered whether the mobile station towers situated close to his residence had anything to do with his frequent headaches! Where in the city could you find a place away from them? But don't they say microwave radiation is not ionising and hence harmless? He wasn't sure. Well, the risk is the price we pay for the convenience and comfort we enjoy, he thought grimly. As if on cue, his cell phone rang. It was his uncle directing him to come home soon.

Prem figured he surely meant 'as soon as possible'. Apparently, there were some legal issues with the family business. Was there a real urgency in his voice that he was disguising by trying to sound calm? But his uncle was a jittery person who got upset over the slightest things. What could be the matter now? He unlocked the phone again and dialled Ramesh. He felt the headache worsening. *Come on, pick up*. It kept ringing and there was no answer. He would be out on the field, supervising, and would have left his phone in the car. As he hurried, Prem tried to control his apprehension.

Within half an hour, he was in a bus headed to his native town. He kept trying to reach Ramesh, his head throbbing with pain now.

* * *

It was late evening when Prem finally arrived home. It was as bad as he had imagined, possibly worse. There had been an accident at Ramesh's workplace. A makeshift platform on a building had collapsed and Ramesh had fallen down from a height of over thirty feet with nothing to break the fall. His condition was critical.

Prem now stood outside the intensive care unit in the hospital, the shock blocking out all other emotions. He felt a hand on his shoulder and turned. It was the doctor, who took him aside and said, "Listen calmly. I'll be straight with this. I'm afraid the prognosis is not good. He is badly hurt. We have done all we could. For a while he has been in and out of consciousness. He wants to speak to you, Prem."

In a few minutes Prem was beside Ramesh's bed. He tried his best not to look at the equipment around or the room itself and focused on his brother instead. Ramesh smiled weakly. Prem reckoned he wanted to talk. He whispered, "Yes, talk to me!" And Ramesh spoke. Prem listened carefully, unable to utter a word. He couldn't give hope to either his brother or to himself. Nevertheless, he knew instinctively his presence was all that Ramesh really needed.

* * *

Prem hopelessly tried to give strength to his parents. A moment ago, the doctor had informed them that it was all over. Now overwhelmed with emotion, Prem desperately made his way to the doctor's room. He collapsed onto a chair and tried to get his bearings.

"Sir, I'm here to carry out his wishes."

"Yes," said the doctor sympathetically and waited.

"Ramesh has whole-heartedly bequeathed his body to the hospital. For medical research. His body is not to be displayed to anybody but our parents. He doesn't want anyone seeing him in this condition..."

"Are you sure about this?"

"Yes." Prem was struggling with himself, but his tone was firm.

"All right. But don't you think you should consider your relatives' opinions too?"

"No. Please do this for me. I know what I am talking about."

"Okay, I'll do my best to fulfil his wishes. Be brave."

* * *

Prem was now at home, staring with unseeing eyes at the people who came to offer their condolences. There were a handful of them who were genuinely concerned. They were really helpful. Most people mumbled something like 'at least he didn't suffer'. After a while, Prem became frustrated. Yes, Ramesh wouldn't have wanted to live in a comatose vegetative state; it was against all his principles. But these people offering advice had no idea of Prem's true feelings. After all Ramesh was *his* brother. The loss directly affected him and his parents. Everybody else could forget it in a few days. Even while wishing he shouldn't suffer, Prem had prayed and hoped for a miracle. He could never accept the fact that his brother might be leaving him. Well, now he had. Left him. Forever.

No final rites were performed for Ramesh, as per his wishes. He had never believed in such things. For him religion was akin to Shakespeare's lines, "If you tickle us, do we not laugh? If you prick us, do we not bleed...?" To help the needy and not hurt anyone. A concern for your fellowmen would make you aware of what makes them laugh or bleed. The decision regarding his mortal remains and the rites had invited protests from the family. Prem had sternly though painfully carried it out. He was fairly tough, yet he was bitterly hurt by their insensitive remarks. He never hesitated to do what he thought was right. None of this was easy for him.

He watched as a few relatives put his father through the mill, trying to get the details of the death. His dad was obviously fraught with agony. As he listened, Prem knew it was neither sorrow nor concern that was driving them to ask such thoughtless questions but a morbid curiosity which got the better of them. When he could stand it no longer, Prem walked over to them and exploded, "Will you just leave him alone?" An elderly lady retorted sharply, "You are the reason the rituals were not performed. His soul won't even be liberated! Did you at least let us see him one last time? Now what is the use of blowing your top?!!"

Adding insult to injury she rambled on, the comments becoming harsh, provocative. Prem decided not to take the bait. Closing his eyes, he tried to remain calm. The 'Bhagavad Gita' said about evil being like water drops on a lotus leaf...for the devoted soul. "*Padmapathramivambhasa*... You be the lotus leaf. Let them try to ruin your composure." He left the room on seeing his father sobbing.

There was something skewed and funny here. It was ironical that some of these folks watched television serials and movies and got so involved that they wept for the characters. But when there was a real tragedy in their own family, they were able to watch it like a movie, detached! *You are overreacting.* Prem reproached himself. He thought of his kith and kin helping them deal with the heartbreak and taking care of things at home. Surely, he shouldn't think ill of anybody. For the past several years he had trained himself that way. Instead of snapping back angrily in case of a disagreement, he tried to imagine himself in the other person's shoes and understand. If someone hurt him he chose not to respond, except for making a silent resolution to avoid doing the same when someday he was in their place. *Let the wounds be buried with my bones.*

A couple of weeks later, Prem knew there was nothing more he could do to alleviate the anguish of his mourning parents. He must now leave it to time to heal them. As he decided to return to his job, he felt hollow inside. Prem realised that a quintessential part of himself had died with Ramesh.

CHAPTER III

Sheela looked up from her computer game suddenly, realising her eyes and neck hurt. Getting up and stretching, she admired the programmers who developed such complex games. Being housebound, in the midst of a scenic location in Kerala, she was getting addicted to these online adventures lately.

A postgraduate in science, she aspired to pursue research abroad. Sheela was always fascinated by the idea of linking the physical sciences with metaphysical and philosophical theories. She had realised from her own experience that the more you learn, the more you comprehend the extent of your own ignorance.

Sheela was all of five feet tall, slight and nimble and a bit socially awkward. She found it difficult to achieve her professional goals. Both her parents were teachers. Though they were always supportive and desired her success, they were apprehensive about sending her far. Most of their friends and relatives had advised her to find a job close to home. "It is the practical aspect that we are telling you," they would start sermonising. "Right now, you feel only the thrill of your youth. That's actually a mirage! What you propose to do is not suitable for a girl." Yet she had well-defined, timebound objectives of working abroad for a few years and then returning to continue her work. She was aware that her parents' friends and colleagues were doing far better in life than they were. Not that she felt any resentment. God had been kind to her. Still, she had this feeling that her parents had never made use of their full potential. She understood it was partly because of their personal problems and partly due to their unwillingness to take any chances to follow their dreams. But they were content with what they had, which was all that mattered. She was conscious that they had endured a lot in their life and had true respect for them. They wanted her to get married and settled in life. Well, if she was not serious about her work or life, how could they expect her to have a commitment to marriage? She found herself tormented with inner conflicts, pondering whether by going with her plans she would be following her selfish interests. Sheela, sometimes looked upon as a rebel, didn't want to dishearten her parents.

Even at school and college, she hadn't quite fitted into most peer groups, for she was in many ways poles apart from them. Occasionally, she would long to be one among them, giggling and chattering and sharing secrets... At times, she too wished to be the exemplary girl. A girlie girl. On the whims of fashion. Knowing how to blush! With secrets to share.

Consequently, Sheela was in no way interested when a proposal for marriage came in. Some guy with an MNC job, from a respected family – a suitable 'alliance' for her. She had heard her parents complain about the difficulties of raising girls, the pressure they were under, the rising prices of gold and so forth. God, was she becoming such a huge responsibility? Well, she shouldn't blame herself for her existence, but that was what she did every time she heard such remarks. *Look at it from their point of view. Try to understand.* She disliked the whole system here and had little respect for the status quo of society. Yet she thanked God that she was not born in one of those war-affected, troubled places with ethnic conflicts and poverty. She couldn't envisage the life of the oppressed people there. Not that she failed to count her blessings. Nonetheless, her independent, individualistic nature made her agitated about things every so often and sometimes earned her repugnance. *Well, those are the conflicts you live with!*

Sheela decided to take a walk outside and enjoy the splendid landscape adorned by mountains and lush greenery.

CHAPTER IV

$\mathcal{P}$rem was seated in front of a computer screen checking the value of the shares he had purchased in the stock market. He was fairly new at this business, trying his hand at it for the past several months. He ran his fingers through his hair contemplating the options. He had been kind of restless ever since Ramesh's second death anniversary a few days back. Time might heal the wounds, but it certainly didn't fill the void! Somehow, he was unable to concentrate on his work. His boss had pointed out that he seemed to be falling behind. He turned back to the LCD screen. On an impulse, he made a speculative investment decision. *This may be risky*, he thought glancing at the figures before him. *Whatever.*

* * *

Inside the almost empty café, Prem was sipping his black coffee. He always took his coffee black, being a vegan, a supporter of animal rights, sometimes being a laughing stock to others. He said no to products like leather, silk and honey. All the killing, trade, sports and testing involving animals seemed cruel to him. He was deeply pained at the sight of animals or birds caged, being transported under pathetic conditions or elephants brought for festivals being tortured. *Laws must be enforced to check all these; and to treat and kill the creatures used as food humanely as they do it in some developed countries.* He knew there were millions of people around the world who shared his views. And so, he remained musing. The child who wouldn't hit a mosquito. The man who refused to drink milk.

A couple of mouth ulcers rendered the process of ingestion difficult for him. He was jolted awake from his reverie by a voice.

"Hello, mind if I join you?"

Prem looked up to see the bright face of a man about thirty, tall and well built, carrying a teacup. Prem was so lost in his thoughts that he hadn't seen the stranger approaching.

"My pleasure," he managed.

"You must be Prem." He sounded vaguely familiar. He continued, "I am a friend of Ramesh. Call me Raj. I've been transferred to our Design and Testing wing here."

"Glad to meet you, Raj," said Prem, trying hard to recollect anything about him that Ramesh might have told him.

As if sensing his uneasiness, Raj went on, "I suppose Ramesh hadn't told you about me. We were out of touch for quite a while. I'm sorry about what happened. Knew you were working here. Been thinking of enquiring in your department when I stumbled upon you. Didn't have much trouble recognising you. You look like your brother!"

Prem's eyes momentarily filled with tears. He blinked them away. The twosome chatted on for a while. Then Raj put his cup down and smiled warmly. "It was nice talking to you. Gotta run now. See you again soon!"

"Sure! I work in the new R&D building near the pool. Let's catch up sometime," said Prem as his brother's buddy disappeared down the hall.

Prem winced in pain, taking another sip of his drink. These mouth ulcers were killing him. Swearing silently, he downed the rest of the coffee.

* * *

Prem waited impatiently for the webpage to refresh. When he gazed at the monitor again he was thrilled. The impulsive choice he had made only weeks before had turned out to be the right one. It was now time to get returns from this investment.

* * *

Prem walked into the cabin, greeting his boss who was obviously pleased to see him. They shared an amiable relationship. Prem was a valuable employee.

"So, what is the new breakthrough?" he asked Prem cheerfully.

"Sir, there is something important I need to talk to you about."

The other man waited.

"I want to quit my job."

"You are kidding!"

"No sir, I'm serious about this."

"May I know why?"

"Personal."

"That is not convincing enough. Is there anything disturbing you, Prem?"

Close as they were, Prem didn't feel the need to elaborate.

"I'm sorry about this. I have to leave."

"At this stage? Are you out of your mind? It's one of the most brilliant and sophisticated ventures we have ever dealt with. A dream project! It'll be the biggest blunder of your professional life."

"Maybe. I apologise."

"We were planning to send you overseas to lead a team onsite. You can't just walk out now. And you do of course realise you are bound by the service agreement regarding this project?"

"I'm sure somebody else can take my place. And I'm prepared to pay the compensation."

Prem walked out of the office before his bewildered boss could even begin to coax him out of it. Though he knew he was not indispensable he felt bad about backing out of a commitment like this. He had never done so before. On the contrary, it had reached a stage where he could no longer do justice to the task at hand. As a result, he'd hardly contributed anything to this classified project they had undertaken. Of course, every member of the team was required to sign a bond regarding this particular project due to its sheer magnitude and confidentiality. He would be required to pay a rather large amount of money in order to quit. But then, the earnings from the stock market combined with a part of his savings would take care of that. He would end the contract.

* * *

Prem met Raj once again on the campus and told him of his plans. Listening carefully, he replied, "A lot of people may tell you that you are ruining the opportunity of a lifetime and all that. But I say, 'Follow your heart'."

Follow your heart. That was what Ramesh used to tell him. Raj said, "I am likely to get a transfer to our branch in Kerala too. See you then."

* * *

Prem was lucky to have a window seat on the bus home. He had discovered that Raj had worked with Ramesh some time back. His family too was in Kerala. There was a warm-hearted quality about him though his demeanour seemed a bit strange. Within the short time he'd spent with him, Prem had got to like him and considered him trustworthy.

As the bus moved on, he spotted a cow grazing by the side of the road. The rope around its neck and through its nose was tied to its forelegs. This was done by the owner to prevent the cow from straying too far. The poor animal, with its head close to its legs, was struggling to move. Prem felt helpless. Taking in the scene, Prem realised that he himself had similar restraints and restrictions albeit not physical ones. He was in the same state as that creature, bound and beleaguered. For a fleeting instant, he had a vivid vision of Ramesh at the hospital battling for life. *Follow your heart.* Yes, he could now feel the energy and derive the inspiration to follow his dreams.

CHAPTER V

A few weeks had passed since Prem returned home. He had found a convenient job in a medium-scale industrial complex about twenty kilometres from home. He sought out a deserving charitable organisation and volunteered to work there.

His parents were both startled and confused at his sudden decision. Firstly, they were not happy about his quitting a well-paid job with a top-notch reputed company. Then there was this particular proposal for marriage for Prem his parents were interested in. They had informed the girl's family that he had a job at an MNC.

His dad was advising him, "The best thing about this proposal is that the horoscopes match well. They are well off and will offer a great deal as dowry…"

"Dowry?" said Prem incredulously. "It is banned! We're not going to take anything."

"Well it is not dowry. They just give you gifts to…"

"I will not accept anything. It is against my principles."

His father sounded hurt, "This is an issue of our prestige as well as theirs. It is a symbol of social status. If we don't accept anything people will assume there is something wrong with the boy! Imagine the criticism and embarrassment! And think of the humiliating disparagement the girl's family will have to put up with."

"Oh! Come on dad. This state is supposed to be literate and modern. Still you hold onto the old practices and care about what people might think. You don't need to hesitate to do what is right."

Prem was lost in his thoughts for a while. Dowry was an ancient system where the bride's parents gave her gifts and money for her own financial independence. Besides, it was presented to her by family and friends as a sign of joy. Initially, dowry was bestowed to the bride and not the groom or his family, until the patriarchal system took over and changed things. Post that, women had fewer legal rights until recently, when new laws were implemented. Despite the new laws, thought Prem, dowry practically remained a norm and menace.

"Well, you do things to give us nothing but pain in our old age! First you give up a nice job for no good reason. Then you disagree to the marriage proposal. We have sacrificed everything for you! We just want to see you settled now…for your own good. With your brother gone, you're the only hope for us to carry on the family name. Why do you want to hurt us so much?"

Prem snapped back, "How am I hurting you? I listen to you. But you pay no heed to my own convictions. Right from childhood, my life has been laid out before me and I have had to follow the path you set. You think that is best for me. Any choice of my own and you are not pleased. Am I doing anything immoral or illegal? Why does it have to be this way?"

Without missing a beat his father answered, "That is what all youngsters tell their elders. You forget it is all for your own benefit. You have no idea how much trouble we go through to keep you happy!"

Prem fell silent; he was filled with remorse. Of course, he did know that. But that was the also the worst tool used for emotional blackmail in the family. It wasn't always fair. Parents sacrifice the major part of their lives to bring up their progeny, not living their own – *At the cost of living their own lives*. Well, that was considered righteous. But the result – expectations; failure to recognise children as individuals with their own views, forcing one's failed dreams on one's children, imposition to tread the path they lay out in the best interests of their offspring; the anxiety that the son or daughter will disgrace them and bring about pain for everyone when they disagree with them. He felt there must be a balance between living your own life and caring for your children.

Try as he might he could never restrain himself while speaking to his folks. All his emotions bubbled out, often leading to arguments. The worst part was the feelings of guilt and self-reproach he had to deal with for days afterward.

The conflict between fulfilling your parents' wishes and doing justice to your own calling.

*   *   *

Prem was heading back home on his motorcycle, fighting an urge to ride like a daredevil. He was content with his new way of life. He was riding back after visiting some patients along with his co-workers at the charitable trust. Initially he had been surprised at how many needy souls lived in and around his place. He had been walking by them every day, ignoring them, unaware of their suffering. In the past few weeks, he'd accompanied his colleagues on their visits to chronically ill patients, poor ones who couldn't afford treatment, young men paralysed overnight in accidents, homeless aged persons, parents who couldn't send their children to school... The list was long indeed. At first, Prem was heartbroken at the pathetic scenario. He wondered how the rescuers and health workers managed to deal with such trauma compassionately and then forget about it past their work shifts. That was the only way to do it, he realised. Later on, the natural leader in him took over and Prem began coordinating the activities of the group, working out strategies.

He accelerated, mulling over his recent experiences. He reflected on the human psychology of wanting more. A sick person yearns only for his good health and nothing else. A poor or homeless man just desires a meal or a roof to sleep under. *If only I could regain my health! If only I have a room to sleep in! If only I earn enough to eat twice a day!* Yet once the primary needs are satisfied, people naturally desire more. A better job. A bigger house. A higher income. Another car. Starting a family. Fame. Prosperity... And even after they had achieved a lot in life they were not content. The wish list was endless. Seldom did you find a person satisfied with what he/she had. This was human nature! It was not just their craving for more; it was also because the social order expected it out of you - to keep on doing more. You might be considered dull and unambitious if you didn't. Once you are healthy you are supposed to be educated; once you are qualified you are expected to find a job and earn; once you do that you are supposed to get married and so on. Whether you liked it or not, you got caught in the tangle of civilisation one way or the other, sooner or later in life. Man was a social being after all; without some degree of societal acceptance, he couldn't survive. As he passed the supermarket, he remembered he needed something. Parking the bike, he started walking the short distance. He was surprised at the person he ran into. Raj.

"Guess you were transferred!"

"Yeah, came down to meet somebody here. Shall we take a walk?"

Raj's company put Prem instantly at ease and he found himself speaking freely to him. About the marriage proposal, Raj said, "Look at it from your parents' point of view. They have certain responsibilities and pressures on them to see to that the wedding is grand. That is why even educated families insist on dowry and extravagant ceremonies. They don't possess the boldness or audacity to diverge from convention and face the consequences. Your parents really want what they think is the best for you."

"All that show! I hate it."

Raj laughed. "I know you do. But it is not just show. It is a celebration. Time for the rest of the family to rejoice, if not you."

"Maybe. But think of the stress it puts on poorer sections of the community or single parents who are forced to keep up with the trend. They are careworn gathering the funds and ornaments for the purpose."

"Well, again, that's the way our society is. Don't you deem dowry to be an initial capital to start your life with?"

"Never. That is grossly unfair."

"I empathise with you, Prem. You can take a stand of your own. I respect your choice. I must go now."

"May I have your new phone number?"

Raj gave it to him.

"Drop by my house someday, Raj."

"Definitely." Raj paced away, hopped into his car and drove off.

Feeling better after the conversation, Prem proceeded to the supermarket. It had been a tiresome day.

CHAPTER VI

$\mathcal{S}$heela got into her Ford, adjusting the seat to suit her short stature. The car had obviously been designed for a bigger person. She drove along the beautiful countryside and towards the town. She was going to meet her prospective groom for coffee at a restaurant. Quite astonishingly, both their families had agreed to their meeting each other on their own, away from home, before proceeding further. It was a relief that they had relaxed the traditional ways a little. Caste, religion and social status were the determinants for these arranged marriages...and yes, the horoscopes.

In about an hour, she found the place and drew up into the parking lot. She got out, ignoring catcalls from a few taunting lads and stares from some strangers. Ladies faced such jeering most of the time even in this supposedly advanced part of the nation. Sheela considered these men mentally underdeveloped as they failed to realise how much they hurt women. Due to these potential dangers, she was advised not to travel alone. She was irritated at these restrictions. But there really was no practical solution to it.

She strode to a table, glancing at her watch. Didn't he say half past four in the afternoon? Then she caught sight of the tall, balding guy with windblown hair alighting from a motorbike, whom she recognised as the one from the photograph.

*   *   *

Prem and Sheela sat on opposite sides of the table weighing each other up. They had discussed their individual interests and plans for about half an hour. Feeling more comfortable now, Sheela went on, "People used to tell me I would never find a groom with my character and build!" She was no stranger to the usual sermons every girl could relate to. In this country, marriage was considered to be the one-stop solution to multiple problems. Curing diseases, bringing discipline to youngsters' lives, support to aging parents, propagating your family name, the ticking biological clock, social status...the list of justifications was endless. The truth was that a lot of people tied the knot not because they were really ready to or wanted to, but to avoid the consequences otherwise. Then they got into the flow, some liking it more than others.

Prem laughed. "And they have been telling me to get married before I lose all my hair!"

"Most guys are obsessed with beauty. Don't you care about that?"

"I don't care about looks. I just care about your outlook. Well, that must sound cheesy!"

"Prem, do you really think talking to each other for a short time is sufficient to make a lifetime commitment?"

"Not really. But what other option do we have here?" He continued, "You know, the modern style of dating might seem better, but it is not without flaws."

"True! But, we are bound by our culture, sometimes way too much. Something may go wrong in a marriage with a random choice of spouses. Even if it is the fault of one partner, both suffer. The social taboos associated with divorce and remarriage still exist. The same system that ensures social security can be a bane in other situations."

"Which ultimately rests with the attitude of the people. Hard to change a mindset and decades of cultural programming."

"Exactly."

"Things are far worse in many parts of the world…"

"We must be thankful."

"Yeah, maybe we can make a difference by reaching out to them. Together." Prem's voice was warm, his tone resolute.

"Yes, I ought to give these facts some thought."

They chatted on for a long while.

Prem suggested, "I am against any ostentation related to the wedding."

"So am I. If we both decide so our people will have to agree," she chuckled.

"But I have been thinking it over for a long time. We can either be headstrong about it, make our families unhappy and be termed as rebels. Or we can just let them rejoice and celebrate this the way they wish. Which would you choose?"

Sheela leaned back, considering this. "Well then, the second one. I guess we owe it to them."

"And we are not going to touch a single paisa out of your wedding endowments... Wait, I have an idea to utilise it in a better way."

"Deal!" Sheela smiled heartily.

They realised they were actually talking about their wedding even before agreeing to it explicitly.

Before parting Sheela said, "Prem, I would like to retain my maiden name after marriage."

"Sound a bit like a feminist, don't you?" Prem teased.

"No, I'm a realist."

"Granted!" His smile was genuine.

* * *

Sheela was thinking hard on her drive back. She had met a lot of men before, some who were potential marriage alliances. Nobody shared her views as the way Prem did. Of course, she still had to finalise her decision. Prem had been receptive to all her ideas, had even encouraged her to follow her dreams. He didn't seem to notice her lack of a sense of style and fashion. She thought of the plans he had conceived – to form a Non-Governmental

Organisation for social causes including a shelter for stray animals. He had a perspective on every matter that was both unconstrained and unconventional. Beneath the calm exterior, Sheela sensed a raging fire of determination and purpose in him.

How could she take a decision about Prem abruptly? That was a major downside with arranged marriages. Both families awaited your answer and they would either set about the wedding preparations or continue the 'alliance' hunt, as the case may be. That was when she had a sudden reminiscence. Her aunt's elder daughter, her cousin, had had a 'love marriage' which the family didn't approve of. After a while there occurred the inevitable marital problems and her aunt rebuked the girl, "It is your own fault! This was all your choice. Now you have to suffer the consequences yourself. None of this would have happened if we were involved." Her second daughter had an arranged marriage and soon similar problems popped up. This time the aunt advised, "This is how life is. Maybe it's your destiny. You must cope with it somehow!" Sheela chortled at the memory. Funny the way they never took the blame upon themselves.

Turning onto the rugged road leading to her house, she switched on the headlights and concentrated on the treacherous dirt path ahead.

CHAPTER VII

Sheela was playing badminton with a friend when her uncle and aunt came to fetch her. She was wanted home urgently and they wouldn't tell her why. In the car, they just told her to be calm. She discerned something was very wrong.

* * *

They reached the hospital in a quarter of an hour. She joined her relatives and neighbours outside the cardiac care unit. Her dad had suffered a cardiac arrest. He had been treated for high blood pressure earlier. Her mother was overwrought with worry. The people around her wouldn't give her any details. When Sheela demanded to know, her uncle came forward. "Not to worry dear. They'll just give him an IV drip and he'll be fine. We will take care of everything." She couldn't believe it. She was twenty-two and they gave her that! Treating her like a three-year-old. She was overcome with pain and anger. She feared for her dad and wanted to know how bad his condition was. Yes, she was grateful to her relatives for being there. But it still hurt. They thought she was too immature to understand and deal with the situation and hence she was denied information on her own father's illness; even so, they thought of her as mature enough to get married and start a family. This was ridiculous! She knew part of it had to do with her being a woman.

Sheela sauntered along the corridor, filled with grief and fury, and sank into a chair. She wanted to see her dad. She realised with bitterness that although her dad had tremendous confidence in her, even he had rendered her incapable of handling certain problems.

* * *

Sheela was able to go in and see her dad as he had asked for her. Later she had gone to seek information from the doctor who was treating him. He didn't really discuss the details with her, suggesting implicitly that she send an uncle or brother to talk about the matter. His condition was serious and she was kept in the dark. Obviously, he too thought she might break down in a crisis. Her looks didn't help either! Sometimes she had no say in issues concerning her.

* * *

Prem was at home dealing with some paperwork. His parents were impatient and anxious about his reply regarding the girl he'd met. Prem liked her frankness and her lack of pretence. They were grilling him for details when they heard that Sheela's father was hospitalised a couple of days back. Prem set off on his motorbike.

* * *

Sheela came out of the hospital room to find a visitor. She was both surprised and relieved to see him. Knowing she was in an emotional turmoil, Prem took her aside and said, "I am not here to console you. I don't think you are a weak person to be comforted in that way. I'm sure you can handle it."

Sheela didn't utter a word. It was the most understanding thing anyone had said to her in the last two days. He went on to say how bad he felt about her dad's condition and concluded with a reassurance, "Whenever you need me, just give a call."

Sheela was thinking of Prem long after he had left. Her kith and kin were very loving and caring. But Prem did something they didn't. *He understood her.* Maybe it was her fault that she failed to communicate effectively with her well-wishers. It was all due to her very disposition. *Stop blaming yourself. You never did as much as think bad of anyone.*

She had to admit that Prem's visit had been most helpful. He had said all the right things. There was no false hope in his words; no consoling tones; no sympathy; no treating her like a kid. Just assurance. She was vaguely aware of the fact that Prem had faced a similar situation when his brother was hospitalised though he had not spoken about it to her.

* * *

Sheela was at home with her family after a few days, her father having made a full recovery. He was well and happy and on medication. Moreover, they had finalised Sheela and Prem's marriage and now kept themselves busy with the wedding preparations.

Her aunt looked at Sheela from head to toe saying, "Put some meat on your bones before the wedding, will you?" Sheela smiled genuinely. As far as she knew, she maintained the optimum weight for her height. All the world was after fitness these days. Only here did they consider you healthy only if you were plump. It was again one of those weird, conventional views in a relatively sophisticated culture and community.

CHAPTER VIII

The wedding ceremony was conducted in all its grandeur and traditional splendour, to the satisfaction of both the families. Prem yielded to everything although it was against his convictions. But so was hurting his parents who had been in a delicate state ever since they lost their elder son. He felt his principles contradicted each other. Therefore, he sacrificed his self-gratification for the pleasure of those around him.

The newly-wed couple moved to an apartment after the wedding. Prem had tried to contact Raj several times and failed. He wasn't surprised. Raj was a peculiar fellow who almost never answered the phone. Even so, Prem realised he hadn't known a more loyal and understanding person before, having met him several times by now. He was the one person who accepted Prem without asking him why his teeth were this way or his hair that way. He laughed at the silly observation. He didn't even admit it to himself that he was hurt when somebody commented on his hair. The problem was that it made him self-conscious. It was Raj's genuine nature that appealed so much to Prem.

Prem and Sheela were having a good time together. She was glad to accompany him on his trips to various infirmaries, prisons and the like. The volunteers at the charitable home were delighted to welcome them. She was more than willing to assist Prem in his work. At the same time, the pair received frequent advice to find better jobs. In fact, when Sheela got a great job offer, Prem wanted her to take it up knowing she had once dreamed of it. But she preferred to opt for a part-time job with a research institution. It was not merely a compromise; she was now honestly interested in his ideas. She promised him she would pursue her passions in due course of time.

* * *

Prem was busy discussing his new endeavours with friends. He counted on them to support him. One evening he bumped into Raj in the city. Quite surprisingly, the two of them met whenever Prem really wished to. Raj congratulated Prem on his wedding and Prem enquired about his job. "Fine," Raj assured him. The duo strode to a snack bar. Prem was disappointed to learn that they didn't serve black coffee. Raj advised him, "Compromise on petty things, but not on values – motivational speaker and author, Shiv Khera advocates this. Otherwise your life will become miserable."

"All right. I'll take it with milk just this once."

Prem didn't know why he always agreed with Raj. Raj declined a drink. They discussed various topics in depth. Prem noticed a waiter throwing curious glances in their direction.

Prem found it difficult to drink the coffee with the mouth ulcers that had appeared again. Suddenly he had a recollection – of a couple of mouth cancer patients they had visited. The treatment made their mouths and throats so dry that they had to put tamarind on the tongue to induce salivation. Hungry, yet unable to eat a grain... Prem was unaware of the tears in his eyes and felt no pain as he gulped down the hot drink.

Raj put a comforting hand on his shoulder. "All your efforts will be fruitful. Just believe in yourself. By the way, how is Sheela doing?"

Prem was jolted back to the present. "Well, I almost forgot. It's her birthday today! Got to run. Care to accompany me? I want to introduce you to her."

"Another time. Miles to go before I sleep!"

And they parted.

* * *

Sheela was waiting for Prem to return home. Now that she was getting to know him better, she understood that he was just as sensitive as he was tough; hypersensitive at times, turning bitter at an unintentional remark. He was undeterred and sentimental all at the same time. She heard the door opening behind her and turned.

Prem greeted her and awkwardly extended a small gift-wrapped box. She unwrapped it to find a gold ring inside.

"So thoughtful of you dear!"

"Like jewellery?"

"Yeah, girls are supposed to like them." In fact, she disliked the fact that people were willing to pay thirty grand for a measly ten grams of gold, but it was considered a waste if you purchased a world-class work of literature for six hundred rupees. Nevertheless, the role it played in Indian culture was undisputed!

"You are no typical girl."

"Well, I like gold from a philosophical point of view," she said sheepishly.

Prem raised his eyebrows.

She continued, "You expose silver or copper to air or water and they get tarnished and corroded. Gold doesn't because it doesn't react with its surroundings."

"It doesn't need to react since it already has a stable structure."

"Exactly. Which is why it's termed a noble metal!" She smiled.

Prem nodded, reminded of the simile of water drops on the lotus leaf.

"Tell me some of your wildest dreams!" Prem queried.

"To drive like a race car driver, to run down the steps of an ascending escalator, to dance in a thunderstorm...and more such crazy stuff. What about you?"

"Close to yours, I guess. Now we are heading to the best restaurant in town."

CHAPTER IX

$\mathcal{P}$rem stopped the car by the edge of a ravine. He had driven to this remote hilly part of the town to deliver medicines to a chronically ill patient. He volunteered to work all his free hours. None of his colleagues were free to go with him today. He got out, breathing the fresh air and started walking along the hillside lined by trees. The mist hung around the mountains and the sunlight filtered through the valleys in an eerie fashion. The atmosphere was captivating. There were a few houses, little more than huts, scattered in the valleys. Many didn't even have access to clean water and electricity. He thought of all the things he took for granted at home. He reached his destination and was heartsick at the sight of the middle-aged man in a wheelchair and his family. More troubling was the look of utter hopelessness on his face which years of suffering had brought upon him.

Prem spoke to him, trying to sound cheerful. He spoke of his own experiences. Then he took leave.

Ramesh would have preferred instant death to such a fate. Prem knew this person did so too. He wiped his eyes. Still, he was intent on bringing what little light he could to these people's lives. He prayed for them.

He almost reached his car. Wasn't that a piece of barbed wire near one of the tyres? The blow came out of nowhere as he bent down to pick it up. He fell sideways, clutching his shoulder. There were three of them, one reaching out and tearing at Prem's pockets. Two of the group looked no more than adolescents. His mobile phone and wallet fell out. He leapt to his feet. The men with the crowbars moved forward. Prem kicked as hard as he could and got one of them. He fought off the others but not without sustaining a few bruises and wounds. He finally got hold of a crowbar and hit an opponent hard across the face, blood spurting out from the lad's face. *The man who wouldn't slap at a mosquito.*

The men scrambled to their feet and slithered down the rocky slopes. Prem stood there dazed, the wind blowing his thinning hair away from his forehead. *The unruffled man with the ruffled hair.*

He managed to get into the car and drive back. He had found his wallet, but his cell phone was gone. He surmised poverty and deprivation could drive youth to do horrendous things.

* * *

It was only later at home that he felt the sharp pangs of pain on his shoulders and arms. The adrenaline had been keeping the pain at bay till now. Sheela was tending to his injuries. "God, you are really hurt."

"Just my ego." He tried to smile. Sheela figured the sensitive part of him was upset while he attempted to act tough.

Later he confided, "I feel so worn out. Even my parents ask me why I can't live like normal people and keep out of trouble. Sometimes I myself feel out of place!"

"You *are* different, Prem. There was this professor in physics in our college who asked us the reason for the difference between the chemical behaviours of neon and sodium. You know, the difference of a single electron can transform an inert gas into a highly reactive…" She looked at him awkwardly.

"All right, I get the point."

"Prem, you are unique and you have a certain purpose in life. So follow your heart."

"I wish the laws are more stringent here so that things will be smoother and safer."

"In a country like ours, everything takes time to bear fruit. There are barriers and opposition everywhere. Implementing stricter laws has its own consequences. Imagine legalising euthanasia or enforcing capital punishment more easily. There has to be a way to ensure that anything done under the rules is just and fair. There is always a chance of misuse."

She continued, "Prem, don't let all this wear out your spirits. In Lincoln's words, only the test of fire makes fine steel." Sheela knew Prem envisioned a world where everyone had a sense of social responsibility. It could be as subtle as closing a tap properly or avoiding illegal parking of a vehicle. All it required was simply a concern for your brethren.

She looked him in the eye and said in a firm voice, "Come what may, I will never leave your side. If there is resistance, we'll face it and face it head on! Together."

He stood up smiling. All he had was bits and pieces of inspiration…and bits and pieces of disappointment. He took hold of her gently and drew her slowly towards him.

CHAPTER X

Prem's plan of establishing an NGO didn't prove to be an easy job. Finding dedicated partners and raising funds were the harder issues. Moreover, the paperwork and the process of registration were painfully slow. He hated the bureaucratic establishment where you had to bribe officials to get things done. Knowledge was light, he observed wryly, but money and political influence constituted the real power. He had learnt it the hard way.

One evening he was inside the office at the industrial complex when Raj turned up. Prem had invited him several times. He told him about the teething troubles he faced.

"Not to lose heart," said Raj. He called up Google on his smartphone, uttering a few keywords. "Take a look at this. See how many people share your views around the globe. You can certainly find likeminded people around you. Now put your resources to good use!"

Prem was astounded to see the number of references to ideas and voluntary organisations and animal rights, some based around where he lived. He gave his word to Raj that he would do his best.

* * *

The very next day, Prem embarked on his mission with a renewed effort along with some good pals. He quit his day job. When he went there to hand in his resignation, one of the cleaning crew told him, "Sir, I thought I heard you speaking to yourself in your office yesterday evening."

"Ah, I might have been on the phone."

* * *

Prem and Sheela set up a website, detailing their vision and made use of social media, receiving an overwhelming response in a month or so. Some of their friends assisted them in many ways. Jointly they called on potential partners and encouraged college students to participate in the mission. Prem and Sheela put their wedding endowments into their funds, thus making efficient use of them. Eventually, the formalities were completed and they finally had an NGO registered for housing desolate people and orphans. They formed tie-ups with schools and hospitals. They obtained buildings and leased out vehicles. The word was spread and the needy approached them. They rehabilitated the destitute and the impoverished. Financial aid was provided for education and medical treatment for the deserving. The whole process took several months. Prem felt the strength in unity. These people, integrated by their shared views and ideas, were now acting in unison.

New members and volunteers joined their organisation with every passing day. At last, Prem pioneered his personal dream of an animal shelter which became his pet venture. They took in stray, diseased or unwanted felines, canines and cattle, nurturing them. His special wing paid visits to pet shops, festivals and zoos. They monitored things within the district, reporting reckless capture, transport, sale or torture of animals and birds, thus freeing creatures that were treated cruelly. Prem had a full task force, consisting of energetic youth, women and students, set up for the purpose. After all, animals formed a part of the planet as much as humans did. While it might be next to impossible to stop all unfairness to them, it was certainly possible to make a huge difference.

* * *

Nine months later, Prem smiled with satisfaction at the success of their joint mission. He was flanked by colleagues at the site where they had started the construction of a new building to cater to their growing needs. Braving the odds, they had accomplished a lot within such a short span of time. His parents were now proud of their son. Sheela had quickly gained popularity in the circle. He appreciated her spirit and commitment.

Ramesh would have beamed with pride at Prem's venture and achievements. He wished Raj was with him. He hadn't heard from him for weeks on end. The guy didn't answer the phone either. Prem had a sudden headache and he felt strange. And then abruptly, he collapsed on the ground.

* * *

Sheela was walking through the mall in the city. She hated shopping, but they were planning something big for their upcoming wedding anniversary. Probably Prem's friend Raj would be joining them too. She couldn't wait to meet Raj, having heard so much about him from her husband. She picked up items, loading the shopping cart, pondering how much Prem had influenced her. She wasn't halfway through the shopping list when she got the news. Prem had been rushed to a hospital and she couldn't understand why.

Disconnecting the call, she hurried back across the shop and through the automatic doors. Hastily she jumped on to the escalator, suddenly realising it was the one going up. She scurried down the steps as if on a treadmill, wryly recollecting what she had told Prem once about her crazy wishes. She hopped into the car and started, manoeuvring the vehicle through traffic. Leaving the city bounds, she let the speedometer climb, driving aggressively, which she would have enjoyed under other circumstances.

* * *

Sheela sat beside Prem on the hospital bed. He had regained consciousness and was able to talk. But something was bothering her; he was acting weird. He was not his usual self at all. They were keeping him under observation.

When his condition did not improve after several hours, Sheela became extremely concerned. Though she remained strong and composed, she wished she could be more rational and less emotional. Then she was informed that the doctor wished to speak to her. Bracing herself, she got to her feet and strode along the corridor to his room.

CHAPTER XI

$\mathcal{P}$rem stood on the balcony staring into the sea; the sun was still too bright to look at. He let the natural beauty and the soothing breeze clear his mind. He was always an admirer of the glorious power of nature. His gaze met the graceful eyes of the burly man next to him. Prem had trouble believing this person beside him was a psychologist. The whole place seemed more like a seaside resort than a shrink's clinic.

There had been a few sessions with him, some which had to be attended along with his wife. This time, Prem had come alone. He had been directed here since he'd had that nervous breakdown. The doctor now faced him. He started in his peculiar voice.

"Prem, you are fully all right now. In fact, you were never really sick. As I told you, the mental breakdown you experienced was merely due to all the stress you were under."

Prem just listened.

"Your brother's demise was the greatest disaster in your life. With that you lost a valuable companion and a friend. You had to deal with a lot of opposition. You arduously strove to implement your plans. Deep within your heart you are very sensitive, which, in a way, explains your profound and innate concern for your fellow beings.

"Through it all, you subconsciously longed for support and recognition; your heart craved for someone who could understand and motivate you. Raj was purely the product of your own imagination. He materialised as that trusted friend you could carry on logical discussions with, someone who provided you practical advice and moral support; someone who cared about you." The doctor paused. "Someone who took the place of Ramesh. In other words, Raj was actually a part of yourself.

"You were truly capable of handling all those problems. Yet your circumstances left you in a more vulnerable, delicate state than you realised, which created the illusion of Raj. It was your mind's way of giving vent to your feelings.

"Now that you have an understanding wife to encourage and love you and assist you in all your endeavours, Raj's presence is no longer necessary. The need for him has vanished from your subliminal mind. So, you don't see him anymore.

"Prem, I congratulate you on your successful mission. You have come a long way, done a great job! Good luck!"

Thanking him profusely, Prem strolled out onto the beach and was immersed in the golden sunlight.

He was engrossed in the magnificence of the gathering twilight. He thought of Sheela. Barely five feet tall. The girl who didn't know how to blush! She had become the love and purpose of his life. She had helped him rediscover himself. As he continued walking towards the car, he failed to perceive the breath-taking beauty of the ensuing sunset over the ocean, for his eyes were now filled with tears.

About the Author

Remya V. Menon is a techie by profession. Writing is her passion; along with penning articles for local magazines, she has recently taken to blogging. She also loves reading, technology, travel, adventure and the outdoors. She believes in making a positive difference, no matter how small. 'Inner Conflicts' is her first book.

You can read her blog at www.remyavmenon.com